The Greentail Mouse

The Greentail Mouse

by Leo Lionni

Pantheon Books

Library of Congress Cataloging in Publication Data

Lionni, Leo, 1910- . The greentail mouse.   Summary: The mice become so involved in their Mardi Gras masquerade they forget it is all in fun. [1. Mice—Stories] I. Title. PZ10.3.L6465Gr [E]   73-1395 ISBN 0-394-82678-7 ISBN 0-394-92678-1 (lib. bdg.)

In the quietest corner of the Willshire woods a community of field mice lived a peaceful life. There were sweet berries, juicy roots, and tender shoots to eat. The winter days were mild, and during the long summer a cool breeze played softly in the grass. No fox or snake ever discovered the hideout where the little friends had a fine time, day after day.

One spring morning a city mouse came passing through.

"Tell us all about the city," the field mice asked him.

"Most of the time it's sad and dangerous," he answered. "But there is one wonderful day."

"When?" asked the mice.

"Mardi Gras," said the city mouse with an air of mystery and importance. "That's French for Fat Tuesday. On Mardi Gras there is lots of music and people dance in the streets." And he told them about parades, confetti, streamers, horns that make funny noises — and masks!

"Let's have a Fat Tuesday too!" exclaimed the mice excitedly.

That very afternoon they met at the big pebble. They all agreed that it would be nice to have a Mardi Gras. "We'll decorate the bushes, we'll have a parade and a ball, and at midnight we'll put on masks."

They worked and worked. They cut leaves into ribbons which they hung from the low branches of trees and bushes. They gathered straw and lichens and petals and made masks of ferocious animals with glittering teeth and fierce eyes.

In the early evening they went to the place they had chosen for the big event. Most of them wore a wig or a hat, and one mouse had even painted her tail green.

"I am the Greentail Mouse," she said with a squeaky voice.

They danced and sang and had a wonderful time until the moon was at its highest point in the sky.

Then they disappeared into the dark bushes and put on their masks. From behind treetrunks and stones they scared each other with ferocious grunts and shouts and shrieks, and threatened each other with sharp teeth and tusks.

Little by little they forgot that they were sweet, harmless mice. They forgot about Mardi Gras and singing and dancing and being joyful. They *really* believed that they were ferocious animals.

"Waoo! Waoo!" yelled the Greentail Mouse from the branch onto which she had climbed.

Everyone was afraid of everyone else, and as the days went by, the once peaceful community became a place full of hate and suspicion.

One morning they saw a strange and frightening sight — *a mouse as tall as the elephant*. A giant mouse! At first they thought that it was a mouse masked as a mouse, but when they realized that it wore no mask at all, they were very frightened and ran as fast as they could. The mouse ran after them, and since he did not have the weight of a mask to carry, he easily overtook them.

"What are you afraid of?" he said. "Have you forgotten what a real mouse is like?"

"But you are the tallest mouse in the world! A giant mouse," the others said, still out of breath.

The mouse laughed. "Nonsense," he said. "If you take off those silly masks you will all be giant mice."

Timidly they removed their masks, one by one, and they realized that the mouse had been right. It was good to be themselves again — real mice, not afraid of one another and anxious to have a happy time.

That night they decided to build a big fire and burn all the masks.

"This is better than Fat Tuesday," they said as the masks turned into ashes, and sparks of many colors rose into the sky.

By the time the fire had died out no one would ever have suspected what had happened, for everything was the way it had been before.

Except for the Greentail Mouse. She just couldn't get her tail clean. She tried the rain and the water in the stream. She scratched and nibbled. She finally gave up. And when someone asked her why she had a green tail, she would shrug her shoulders and simply say, "I was the Greentail Mouse at Mardi Gras."

"What is Mardi Gras?" the other would ask.

"That's French for Fat Tuesday." And she would tell about parades, streamers, and horns that make funny noises. But she never said a word about the ferocious masks. They were tucked far away in her memory, almost forgotten, like a bad dream.